The Tears of the Dragon

By HIROSUKE HAMADA
Illustrated by CHIHIRO IWASAKI
English version by ALVIN TRESSELT

This book translated from *Ryuno Me No Namida*
originally published by Kaisei Sha, Tokyo, Japan.

PARENTS' MAGAZINE PRESS · NEW YORK

Once in the far land of Japan
there was a small village by the edge of a broad river.
The people of the village were gentle and peace-loving,
but they lived with a great fear.
Long ago they had been told that in the craggy mountains
nearby there lived a monstrous dragon. The dragon had
big fierce eyes and a huge mouth that was split
from ear to ear. Out of his mouth flickered a crimson-red
tongue and a breath that was like fire and smoke.

All these things the people had been told, but in truth
no one had ever really seen the dragon. However, these
were simple folk, and they readily believed every word.
Whenever the children of the village were not behaving,
some old man would be sure to wag his finger and warn
them that the dragon was just waiting to snatch them away.
"Is there really a dragon?" the children would ask.
"Will he really come after us?"
"So I have been told by my grandfather's grandfather,"
the man would reply. "And who am I to doubt such a wise man?
The dragon also enjoys eating children," he would add.
In this way the fear was passed from one to another.

But there was one child in the village
who was not like all the others. His name was Akito.
"Who has ever seen this dragon?"
he asked. "Has he ever really
carried off a naughty child?"
The old people just shook their heads.
"That boy will come to no good end,"
they said. "Why, he will undoubtedly
be the first one the dragon will take."
They could not understand this strange boy.

Late one night his mother was awakened
by the sound of the boy crying.
She rushed to his bed
to see what was the matter.
"What is it, my son?" she asked.
"Did you have a bad dream?
Do you have a pain somewhere?"
Akito just shook his head.
"It's the dragon," he told her.
His mother laughed.
"You have no need to fear the dragon,"
she said. "He never bothers
a good and gentle child."
"But I'm not afraid of him," Akito replied.

At this point his mother was puzzled.

"Then why do you cry so bitterly?" she asked him.

"Because I am sorry for the dragon," said Akito.

"Sorry for the dragon?" The mother could
scarcely believe her ears.

"Everyone tells terrible stories about him,"
he went on, "but nobody has ever seen him. Perhaps
he is not a bad dragon at all. Perhaps he even
loves children and does not eat them."

The poor mother did not know what to say, so she
wiped away his tears and tucked him back in bed.

"Do not waste your time feeling sorry for the dragon,"
she said. "The wise men of the village have told us
these things, and surely they must know."

Kissing her son tenderly, she went back to her bed.

Not long after, the time for Akito's birthday drew near.
His mother spoke to him about it, and asked him
if he would like to invite some friends
for his birthday celebration.
Instantly he replied, "The dragon!
I would like the dragon of the mountain
to come to my birthday!"
At once his mother became angry.
"You must stop this dragon nonsense," she said.
"He is a wicked creature, and if you continue behaving
in such fashion you may well see the dragon
sooner than you think. He will come and
snatch you away, and then what will you do?"

In the face of his mother's anger, Akito fell silent.
The days slowly passed. At last it was the third day
before his birthday.
Slipping quietly out of the house before the sun
was barely over the treetops, Akito set out
across the broad fields toward the mountain
where the dragon lived. All day he walked,
and when evening came, he was in the high meadows
of the mountains.

By now he was very tired
and very hungry.
He found a few wild peaches, and he
greedily ate them for his supper.
Then he nestled down at the base
of a large tree and slept.
Early the next morning he was
awakened by the happy songs
of the mountain birds.
Gathering some more peaches
and some raspberries that grew
nearby, he ate them for breakfast.
Then once more he started out
in search of the dragon.

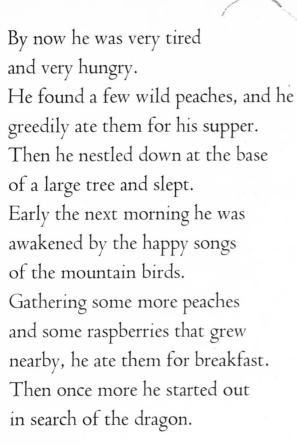

The going grew more difficult
as he climbed higher
and higher
up the craggy mountain.
A bush warbler sang sweetly
and a crow cawed noisily
from the top of a tall
cypress tree.
As Akito passed
through the dark forest
the breeze shook the dewdrops
down upon him
like a gentle rain.

At last the forest ended, and the boy found himself
standing in the sunlight high on a craggy rock,
with nothing but a yawning chasm before him. Everything
was silent. No birds sang, no wind blew in his ears,
and all he could hear was the thumping of his own heart.
"Hello!" he cried in a loud voice. "Hello! Hello!"
And distantly, from across the gorge,
his echo answered: *Hello! Hello! Hello!*
"Perhaps this is the place to rouse the dragon,"
Akito thought, so standing as tall as he could he shouted,
"O dragon of the mountain, where are you?"
And the echo replied: *Where are you? Where are you?*
Where are you? growing fainter and fainter each time.

It so happened that Akito had indeed come near
to the cave where the dragon was sleeping.
It had been so long since a human voice
had been heard in that high place
that the dragon awoke instantly.
"Who is it?" he roared. "Who dares to disturb
the great dragon of the mountain?"
Any other child would surely have been
frightened half to death to hear such a roar.
But of course Akito was not like any other child.
He turned, and there to one side was a cave
with fire and smoke curling out of it.
He was delighted to find that he had reached
the home of the dragon.
"It is Akito from the village by the
broad river," he replied bravely.
"Come out so that I may see you."
"Hmmmm," thought the dragon,
"that is the voice of a child."
And he began to uncurl his scaly body.

With much effort he crawled out of his black cave
into the sun. Akito, his heart pounding with excitement,
carefully studied the dragon. He was just the way
the old people of the village had described him.
His eyes were shining bright and fierce, and his
crimson-red mouth was split from ear to ear.
"Why do you come into this high mountain to see me,"
he demanded, "when everyone knows I am such a monster?"
"I do not believe that you *are* such a monster,
and I have come to invite you to my birthday celebration,"
answered the boy. "Please come. Then the children will
know that they have nothing to fear from you."

Upon hearing this the dragon was very bewildered.
No one had ever spoken to him in such a manner.
"Would it be all right?" he asked, lowering his voice.
"Even though I am so frightening to look upon?"
"Oh yes," replied Akito. "I will see to it
that everyone treats you kindly."
For long minutes the dragon looked at the boy.
Suddenly, in the fierce, piercing eyes of the dragon
a gentle spark flickered. It was a strange spark,
as if it had been imprisoned at the bottom of his
eyes for hundreds of years.

"Thank you," said the dragon softly. "Thank you,
little boy," and he bowed his head before the child.
"Until this time I have never been spoken to kindly by
people. I have been feared and hated for more years
than you have hairs on your head."
His eyes began to fill with tears.
"That is why I, in turn, have always hated people.
I glared in a terrifying manner, and I gnashed my teeth.
When I breathed it was with fire and smoke.
I was, truly, a dragon to be feared.
But now, because of your trust and love,
I feel my hatred draining out of me."

And the tears from the dragon's eyes fell even faster,
until there was a flood upon the ground.
Quickly Akito scrambled up to a tree branch.
"O dragon," he cried, "your tears are becoming
a river. I will surely be washed away and drowned!"
"Climb onto my back," said the dragon.
"Then you will be quite safe."

And in truth the dragon's tears did become a great
flowing river. The blue sky and the high mountains
were reflected on its broad surface,
and the dragon floated on the river like a boat.
Paddling his feet, he sailed along, with the happy boy
perched on his scaly back.
So they went, until the river of dragon's tears
flowed into the broad river in the valley.

Then, as they approached the village, a most peculiar
thing happened. Bit by bit, the dragon's body changed
its shape. It grew longer and narrower, and
under Akito's very feet the creature turned into a boat!
Great clouds of smoke came shooting forth
from his nostrils.

The growl of the dragon grew higher and higher
until it became the happy *toot! toot!* of a boat whistle.
The people of the village were amazed to see
this beautiful dragon boat approaching the shore.
But they were even more surprised to see Akito
standing proudly in the boat.

"Look!" they cried. "It is the strange
child who doesn't believe in our dragon!"
Akito waved happily to the villagers.
"Do not fear the dragon ever again.
Your horrible monster is gone," he called.
"See—instead of the dragon snatching
me away, I have brought him back
for us all to love and enjoy!"